This is Trevor and his dog, Streaker.

She's a hundred-mile hurricane on four legs!

But is she fast enough to go for GOLD?

Jeremy Strong once worked in a bakery, putting the jam into three thousand doughnuts every night. Now he puts the jam in stories instead, which he finds much more exciting. At the age of three, he fell out of a first-floor bedroom window and landed on his head. His mother says that this damaged him for the rest of his life and refuses to take any responsibility. He loves writing stories because he says it is 'the only time you alone have complete control and can make anything happen'. His ambition is to make you laugh (or at least snuffle). Jeremy Strong lives near Bath with his wife, Gillie, four cats and a flying cow.

Are you feeling silly enough to read more?

BATPANTS!
THE BEAK SPEAKS
BEWARE! KILLER TOMATOES
CARTOON KID
CARTOON KID – SUPERCHARGED!
CARTOON KID – STRIKES BACK!
CHICKEN SCHOOL
CHRISTMAS CHAOS FOR THE HUNDRED-MILE-AN-HOUR DOG
DINOSAUR POX
DOCTOR BONKERS!
(A Cosmic Pyjamas Adventure)
GIANT JIM AND THE HURRICANE
THE HUNDRED-MILE-AN-HOUR DOG
THE HUNDRED-MILE-AN-HOUR DOG GOES FOR GOLD!
KRANKENSTEIN'S CRAZY HOUSE OF HORROR
(A Cosmic Pyjamas Adventure)
KRAZY COW SAVES THE WORLD – WELL, ALMOST
LOST! THE HUNDRED-MILE-AN-HOUR DOG
MY BROTHER'S FAMOUS BOTTOM
MY BROTHER'S HOT CROSS BOTTOM
THERE'S A PHARAOH IN OUR BATH!

JEREMY STRONG'S LAUGH-YOUR-SOCKS-OFF JOKE BOOK
JEREMY STRONG'S LAUGH-YOUR-SOCKS-OFF EVEN MORE JOKE BOOK

LAUGH YOUR Socks off with Jeremy STRONG

The Hundred-Mile-An-Hour Dog

Goes for GOLD!

Illustrated by Rowan Clifford

PUFFIN

PUFFIN BOOKS

Published by the Penguin Group
Penguin Books Ltd, 80 Strand, London WC2R 0RL, England
Penguin Group (USA) Inc., 375 Hudson Street, New York, New York 10014, USA
Penguin Group (Canada), 90 Eglinton Avenue East, Suite 700, Toronto, Ontario, Canada M4P 2Y3
(a division of Pearson Penguin Canada Inc.)
Penguin Ireland, 25 St Stephen's Green, Dublin 2, Ireland (a division of Penguin Books Ltd)
Penguin Group (Australia), 250 Camberwell Road, Camberwell, Victoria 3124, Australia
(a division of Pearson Australia Group Pty Ltd)
Penguin Books India Pvt Ltd, 11 Community Centre, Panchsheel Park, New Delhi – 110 017, India
Penguin Group (NZ), 67 Apollo Drive, Rosedale, Auckland 0632, New Zealand
(a division of Pearson New Zealand Ltd)
Penguin Books (South Africa) (Pty) Ltd, 24 Sturdee Avenue, Rosebank, Johannesburg 2196, South Africa

Penguin Books Ltd, Registered Offices: 80 Strand, London WC2R 0RL, England

puffinbooks.com

First published 2012
003

Text copyright © Jeremy Strong, 2012
Illustrations copyright © Rowan Clifford, 2012
All rights reserved

The moral right of the author and illustrator has been asserted

Set in Baskerville
Made and printed in Great Britain by Clays Ltd, St Ives plc

British Library Cataloguing in Publication Data
A CIP catalogue record for this book is available from the British Library

ISBN: 978-0-141-33996-2

www.greenpenguin.co.uk

ALWAYS LEARNING   **PEARSON**

For my grandson, Sam

Contents

1. I Have NOT Got a Girlfriend!

You'd think Streaker was
ill, the way she's been
lying on my bed. Every
so often she lifts her head
a little, looks at me with
the saddest eyes ever, lets
her head fall back on
the duvet, and groans –

HURRRRRRRR. You might even think she was
on the brink of death. She would certainly like
you to think that she's dying. Maybe I should
call an ambulance. On the other hand maybe I
should call a film director – Streaker is such an
actress.

In actual fact *I'm* the one that's ill. I've got a
virus infection. I think every time there's been

anything wrong with anyone in my family our doctor has said: 'It's a virus infection.' Are you limping? It's a virus infection. Your head's exploded? It's a virus infection. I reckon I could be a doctor quite easily if that's all you ever have to tell anyone.

Anyhow, I've been in bed for three days and haven't been to school. I've had to miss Sports Day so I've been pretty fed up. Streaker's been in bed with me. Well, she's been *on* the bed. Every so often Mum or Dad comes upstairs to see how I am. Sometimes they take my temperature and Streaker looks very hopeful. She'd like to have her temperature taken too. Maybe she's got a virus infection. In fact I think Streaker quite possibly *is* a virus infection, on four legs.

It's quite nice to have her up here with me, but she weighs a ton! It's difficult to get comfortable when you've got a large dog slumped across you, especially as she slowly moves up your body. First she was on my knees. Then she shuffled up to my hips. Several minutes later she was across my chest and just now I dozed off and only woke up because she was climbing on to my head.

But, boy, am I bored! I play games on my console, but can't concentrate. I read for a bit, but can't concentrate. I stare at the ceiling. I wait for someone to visit. Tina hasn't been here for ages. Tina is my best friend. (NOT girlfriend – just a friend.) She lives round the corner from me and she's got a dog too. He's a huge St Bernard called Mouse. Ha ha. Does the dog think that's funny? I don't know. Can dogs laugh? Interesting question. These are the kind of pointless things that occur to you when you are lying in bed and getting UTTERLY BORED!

So there's no Tina to cheer me up. Instead I listen to Mum downstairs, going nowhere on her cycling machine. Rumble, rumble, rumble. She even managed to crash the other day! How can you crash a gym-cycle?

'I wasn't looking where I was going, Trevor,' she told me.

'Mum, you weren't going anywhere!'

'I think that's what the problem was. I tried to turn a corner that wasn't there and fell off. I think I've hurt my knee.'

Poor Mum! Anyhow, it's probably only a virus infection, says Doctor Trevor.

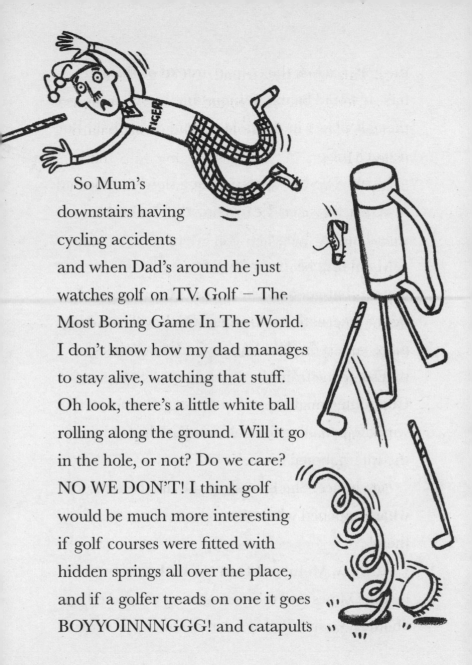

So Mum's downstairs having cycling accidents and when Dad's around he just watches golf on TV. Golf – The Most Boring Game In The World. I don't know how my dad manages to stay alive, watching that stuff. Oh look, there's a little white ball rolling along the ground. Will it go in the hole, or not? Do we care? NO WE DON'T! I think golf would be much more interesting if golf courses were fitted with hidden springs all over the place, and if a golfer treads on one it goes BOYYOINNNGGG! and catapults the golfer across the course instead of the golf ball. It would be much more fun if you had to get the golf player in the hole instead of the ball! But no such luck.

Meanwhile I'm upstairs being slowly suffocated by a dog. Streaker! I can't breathe! You are squashing my lungs!

My mum's been very busy recently on her bicycle-that-goes-nowhere. She's been inspired by the International Games, which will be taking place very soon. I reckon my mum believes that someone from the International Selection Committee might spot her through our front window, pedalling for gold, and ask her to join the International team.

Fat chance! She'll crash at the first bend. Look what happened when the corner wasn't even there!

Anyhow, Mum and Dad are both very excited by the Games and they are getting all worked up about it because in our town we have our very

own International athlete.
He's called Kriss Okonjo
and he is brilliant at running
the 3,000-metre steeplechase.
By 'brilliant' I mean he can
run 3,000 metres faster than
anyone else in the whole
of the United Kingdom.
So that's pretty fast, isn't it?
And maybe, MAYBE, he
might win the International
steeplechase and then he will
be the fastest 3,000-metre
runner IN THE WHOLE
WORLD. That's pretty cool, if you ask me.

And this is even cooler – we're going to the
Games! We've got tickets for the race that Kriss
Okonjo is in, and Tina is coming too! It's going
to be SO exciting!

Anyhow, like I was saying, I was in bed, faced
with two choices. I could either die of boredom

or die of being suffocated by Streaker. Just then there was a terrible din from downstairs. I thought Mum must have ridden her bike straight into the kitchen cupboard.

SPLANGG! SQUINGG! CLANKETTY-PINGG!

But it wasn't Mum at all. It was Tina arriving on her skateboard and thundering at full speed into our rubbish bin. She

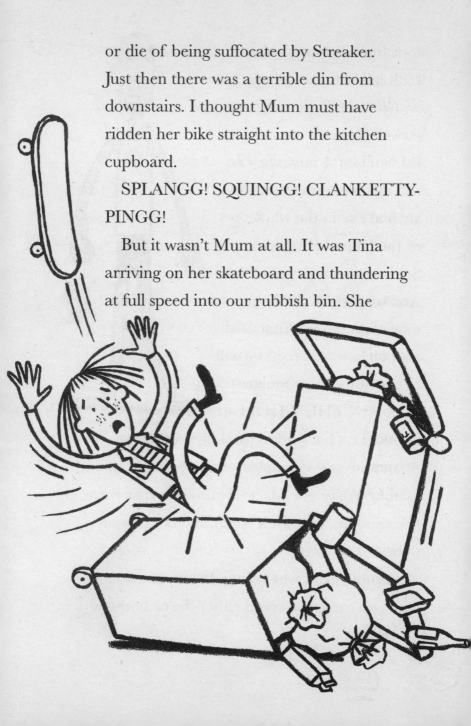

made such a noise even Streaker managed to lift her head for a few seconds and then – *HURRRRRRRRR!* – big sigh, and she dropped back to the bed.

Then there came the *THUD THUD THUD* of Tina taking the stairs two at a time. *BANGGG!* My bedroom door burst open and Tina exploded into the room, yelling.

'Internationalsandeveryonethewholetownsaysin paperandcanalltakepartforanimalsandMouse weightliftingandgoldmedalsandeverythings brilliantfantasticexcitedMumsays!'

'Could you say that again?' I asked quietly.

So Tina took a deep breath and –

'Internationalsandeveryonethewholetownsays inpaperandcanalltakepartforanimalsand–'

'SLOW DOWN!' I shouted. 'Tell me s-l-o-w-l-y.'

Tina sat on the end of my bed and grinned. She's got a grin like sunshine. It always cheers me up.

'You know our local newspaper? It says that the town council has decided to celebrate the International Games by holding their own International Games, right here, in our town.'

That seemed very strange to me. 'But, Tina, hang on, surely all the athletes will be at the real International Games,' I pointed out.

Tina rolled her eyes as if I was being blindingly stupid. 'It's not for athletes, you idiot. It's for animals.'

'ANIMALS?' My mind boggled. It had never done so much boggling. It had almost boggled right out of my ears. I was already imagining elephants going for the long jump and whales bouncing off diving boards.

'Yes,' beamed Tina. 'It's going to be an Animal Games for pets from our town. My mum says Mouse can take part. Streaker could too!' She reached out and patted Streaker's head. 'Just think, Trevor, Streaker might get a gold medal. She could become a doggy Kriss Okonjo!'

The doggy Kriss Okonjo lifted her head for a moment and gazed at Tina with melting eyes. Her head slumped back on to the bed and she groaned. '*HURRRRRRRRRRRR . . .*'

2. Very Fast Cars and Very Fast Dogs

Maybe I was getting better anyhow, but Tina's visit really perked me up. And, when I perked up, Streaker did too. Tina whizzed off home to grab the newspaper and came scooting back, crashing into the refuse bin AGAIN.

Mum came out to see what all the noise was about, just as I wandered down the stairs.

'Oh, it's you, Tina,' said Mum. 'Do you have to make so much noise on arrival?'

'Hi!' Tina beamed back at my mum. 'How's your knee?'

'It's a virus infection,' I shouted down the stairs. They both looked at me as if I was mad. 'Just my informed medical opinion,' I shrugged.

Mum rolled her eyes and changed the subject. 'Trevor – you're up. You must be feeling better.

Three days off school and now you've got half-term ahead of you as well and suddenly you're better. Hmmmm. Some people might be suspicious.'

'Mum, I've been ill. You know I have. Anyhow, Tina says there are going to be Animal Games in town. Have you read about it? Streaker could take part.'

Streaker looked at us with shiny eager eyes. At least they looked eager and shiny to me.

But Mum was aghast. 'Streaker? Take part? Trevor, that dog of yours has never done a single thing that's been asked of her. She is completely untrainable. A carrot is more obedient than that dog.' And Mum went humphing off with her eyebrows somewhere around the top of her head in utter disbelief at the state of things, especially Streaker – and me.

Actually, it's interesting that whenever Streaker does something BAD then she is MY dog. When she does something clever (and I admit it's usually by pure chance that this happens), but, WHEN she does do something clever, suddenly Streaker is OUR dog, according to Mum and Dad. Anyhow, since when has anyone tried to train a carrot to do anything? Have you ever seen a carrot mowing the grass? Ever seen a carrot reading the news on TV? Of course not.

Tina and I went through the newspaper, looking for information. The organizers had invented a whole series of animal games. For example, there was showjumping for horses and rabbits (separate events).

'Rabbits don't go showjumping!' I exclaimed, but Tina nodded and said that her cousin, Archie, had a jumping rabbit. 'And he's really good at it,' she added. 'He'd be great at showjumping.'

'Hey, look at this!' I yelled. 'This is perfect for Streaker – discus for dogs. Only the dog doesn't throw the discus – it catches it! Someone throws a frisbee and the dog has to catch it. I bet Streaker could do that. What are you going to enter Mouse for?'

Tina frowned. 'Shaggiest dog? Laziest dog? Fattest dog? Heaviest dog? Dog-that-doesn't-move-the-longest dog?'

I nodded. 'He'd win all those.'

We scoured the list of events. There was dog racing – which was perfect for Streaker. There was wheel-racing for hamsters, maze-running for rats, a donkey tug o' war and a highest climb for cats. There was even a stay-still-the-longest contest for stick insects.

And then I saw it. Skateboarding for dogs.

'Tina – this is perfect for Streaker! Look!' I showed her the paper.

'Skateboarding? When did Streaker last go skateboarding?'

'She hasn't. But we can teach her. We've got time.'

Tina still needed convincing so I went on. I reckoned a bit of flattery might help.

'You're pretty good at skateboarding. You could help me. You're brilliant.'

Tina gave a little smile. 'Not really,' she began.

I nodded emphatically. 'Yeah – you really are. You can do all those tricks and stuff.'

'What tricks?' she asked.

I was about to say *like crashing into rubbish bins*, but I knew that would be a big mistake. I grinned and said, 'I think your best trick is probably not falling off.'

Tina laughed and punched me playfully. 'You!' she said and gave me THAT LOOK.

Uh-oh. Danger! I backed off hastily. You know what I mean by THAT LOOK, don't you? It's the one where a girl's eyes go all heart-shaped and soppy. Like I said just now, Tina is JUST A FRIEND. Unfortunately, she has other ideas! So I smiled brightly and suggested we started straight away.

'We'll have to get her used to being on a skateboard first of all. I'll tie this bit of string to the front and then we'll pop Streaker on-board and tow her along.'

It sounded dead easy. It looked dead easy too. Put the dog on the board, pull her along. Simple-pimple. Ha ha! How wrong could I be? I should have known Streaker would play up. She just did not want to get on-board. I'd put her on, she'd jump off. I'd put her back and she'd jump off. Put her on. Jump off. On, off. On. Off.

Finally we just stared angrily at each other.

Tina suggested supergluing her paws to the board. Obviously she didn't mean it, but it certainly would have helped. And then, while we were standing there scratching our heads, Streaker climbed on to the board, slumped down, lowered her chin and went 'HURRRRRRRRR', in that sad way of hers.

'It's better than nothing,' I told Tina, and grabbed the string. We set off along the pavement, with Streaker looking as if she was fast asleep. Round the corner we went and who should be coming in the opposite direction?

Charlie Smugg. Charlie Smugg AND his three Alsatians AND his girlfriend, Sharon Blenkinsop. They were blocking the pavement. We would either have to go through them or out into the busy road and round them.

Charlie came up close and stopped. He's an ugly mug, that's for sure – an ugly, very spotty mug. He's fourteen and heavily built, like his dad. (I don't mean his dad's fourteen as well. I mean they're both big. Charlie's dad is the local policeman – Sergeant Smugg.)

'Look who it is,' smirked Charlie. 'It's the two little lovebirds.'

That was pretty rich coming from Mr Smarmy-pants-who-we-caught-kissing-his-girlfriend-once. Not that I could say that to him. He would have killed me.

Sharon giggled, wrinkled her nose and repeated it. 'Lovebirds!' she sniggered, while Charlie's Alsatians tugged at their leads and snarled at Streaker.

Streaker wasn't bothered. She knew she could outrun those Alsatians any day.

Charlie spotted the newspaper Tina was carrying.

'You ain't gonna take part in them Animal Games, surely?' he demanded. 'I wouldn't bother if I were you. Sharon and me – we're gonna clean up. Gonna win everything.'

'You can't win everything,' Tina pointed out. 'You haven't got enough pets.'

'I've got three Alsatians,' he snapped back.

'Streaker's faster than your Alsatians,' I said.

Charlie knew this was true because they had chased Streaker once and she got away – easily. But Charlie just smiled.

'Maybe,' he sneered. 'But Sharon here – she's got a greyhound. An ex-racing greyhound. It's won medals an' everything. Know what he's called?' Charlie leaned forward and almost spat the name at us. 'Lamb.'

Huh! What was so special about that? Charlie nodded emphatically and his sneer grew even more sneery.

'Want to know what that's short for? Eh? Lamb? Wanna know, do you?' He leaned forward again. 'Lamborghini. Yeah. Understand now, do you? Lamborghini. That's a car, that is. Very fast car. That's why the dog's called Lamborghini, cos he's a very fast dog. A great deal faster than that snotty mutt of yours there.'

We all looked down at the skateboard. Streaker opened one sleepy eye for a moment, shut it and went – 'HURRRRRRRRRR'.

3. Run, Run, Run –
As Fast As You Can!

I had been looking forward to the Animal Games
until we bumped into Charlie. He's always BAD
NEWS, if you ask me – a bit like a nasty virus.
Maybe that's Charlie's problem. He's a walking
virus.

Anyhow, the weekend came and Tina and I
were on dog-walking duty. Actually, Tina and I
are on dog-walking duty almost every day. I think
that's why parents have children – so they can
do the jobs parents don't want to do themselves.
You know – mow the grass, walk the dog, feed
the cat, wash the elephant. OK, maybe not the
elephant, but I bet if your parents really did have
an elephant you'd be the one who had to wash
it, cut its toenails and polish its ears. It's a good

thing I like animals, that's all I can say. I'm just a
slave really.

In fact I don't mind walking Streaker. At least
it gets me away from other jobs in the house.
Besides, Tina and I usually go together and we
scoot off to the big fields at the end of my road.
There are some small woods there and a network

of paths you can wander along. It's Streaker's favourite hunting ground. She goes whizzing off after rabbits and squirrels. Mind you, she's never caught anything except a few fleas.

I was worrying about Charlie Smugg, or, rather, I was worrying about Sharon's Lamborghini – the greyhound we had never seen. I was used to Charlie boasting about everything under the sun, but what if Sharon really did have a racing greyhound? A dog that had won medals and everything?

By this time we were heading towards the woods. We'd almost reached them when a tall runner came bursting out from among the trees, took a few steps, stopped dead and checked his watch. Tina stared at him. She nudged me, hard.

'That's Kriss Okonjo!' Tina blurted.

'I know!' I hissed back.

'What's he doing here?' she asked.

I gave a helpless shrug. 'Looking for his trousers?'

'It's KRISS OKONJO!' Tina repeated, as if she might be dreaming, but at that moment the runner looked up and gave a tired grin. He was breathing heavily from all his running.

'Time check,' he said, shaking his head at his watch. 'Got to get faster. Got to get faster.'

'Are you training here?' I asked, and Tina's jaw dropped.

'You spoke to him! You spoke to KRISS OKONJO!'

Kriss gave Tina a broad smile. 'And what's your name, miss?' he asked.

Tina's jaw moved, but no sound came out.

'That's Tina,' I explained. 'I'm Trevor. The big hairy dog is hers. He's called Mouse. My one's Streaker. She's whizzing around here somewhere. If you see ears flapping above the grass, that'll be her.' Kriss smiled, so I went on. 'I thought you'd be training at the running track.'

Kriss scowled and rolled his eyes. 'Have you seen how many people are down there? It's full

of press photographers and journalists. They keep pestering me with questions. *"Hey, Kriss, do you think you can beat Azi Numa? Who do you think is going to win? You or Azi Numa?"* Those reporters just keep banging on about our rivalry.'

I knew this was true. I'd seen it on telly. Kriss

and Azi had been rivals for a long time, even though they both ran for Britain. Sometimes one won, and sometimes the other, but now they were both up for the big one – international gold. And of course everyone in our town was rooting for our local hero – Kriss Okonjo.

Kriss looked pretty fed up. 'I came to train in these woods because it's quieter. I thought the ground out here would help, what with branches sticking out that I have to jump over and puddles to get across. That's what the steeplechase is all about. It's supposed to be a bit like a cross-country race, only without the country. It doesn't seem to be working though. I can't get my times any faster at all.'

'Maybe Streaker can help,' I suggested. 'She can run really fast. You could hold on to her lead. I bet she'd make you run faster.'

Tina had got her voice back. 'Are you serious? Streaker can't help. Kriss is an international runner, not a dog-walker!'

Kriss looked hard at Streaker, who had just turned up and was now sitting very neatly, with her front legs together and her eyes all bright and shiny. She was a picture of helpful innocence. Some people are easily fooled, and Kriss was about to become one of them.

'Could be worth a go,' murmured Kriss. 'I'll do anything to get my time faster.' He slipped his watch from his wrist and handed it to me. 'Here, press this one when I start, and then again when I finish. I need to beat eight minutes and six seconds. Hand me the dog leash.'

Kriss took hold of Streaker's lead. She jumped to her feet at once, ready for the off. You can always tell she's ready by the way her tongue waggles from one side of her mouth. I gave them a countdown.

'Three, two, one – GO!'

Both runners launched themselves down the path. Off they went at lightning speed, with Streaker pulling Kriss behind her. Tina and I

watched as they disappeared round the
edge of the woods. We sat down by the
path and waited, eyes on Kriss's watch.

'Are you sure this is a good idea?' asked
Tina.

'We'll see when they get back,' I
answered.

She grinned at me. 'I can't believe
we're helping Kriss Okonjo!'

'I don't suppose he can believe it
either. Come to think of it, I can't believe
that Streaker is helping him!' We burst
out laughing.

Two figures appeared on the path

coming from town. A shiver ran down my
spine. I recognized them at once. 'Watch out,'
I whispered to Tina. 'Charlie Smugg and his
girlfriend are coming this way.'

Charlie loomed over us, his spotty face
grinning from ear to ear. 'Look who it isn't. Two
little lovebirds.' He pursed his lips and made
kissy-kissy noises at us. He is SO stupid!

'Ooooh, Charlie!' squealed Sharon. 'You are
funny!'

Funny? Charlie? He's about as funny as finding
half a slug on your salad.

'You're the one with a girlfriend, Charlie,' Tina
said quietly. He ignored her and stood there,

gazing around in all directions.

'Have you seen anyone out here running?'

'Running?' I repeated, giving him a blank look. 'Are you trying to catch someone?'

'Thought there might be someone out here running, that's all,' sniffed Charlie. 'Anyhow, where's your crazy dog? Run off again, has she?' He gave a sneery laugh. 'Hurr hurr hurr!'

'You could say that.' I smiled at him.

Sharon pulled a face and hung on to Charlie's arm. 'Charlie, you said we'd get his autograph. You said, Charlie. You promised you'd get his autograph for me.'

Tina brightened up. 'Actually, come to think of it, we did see someone earlier, and he was running.'

'Yeah?'

'It was in the distance. He went that way.' Tina pointed in the opposite direction to the one Kriss had taken.

'Right,' Charlie said, dragging Sharon with

him. 'Come on. Hurry up! What kind of shoes do you call those?'

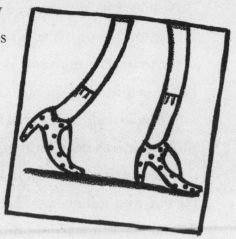

'They're high heels, Charlie. I thought you'd like them.'

'Just get a move on. Hurry up. We'll catch up and get his autograph.' And off they went in the wrong direction, with Sharon whining and Charlie complaining and both of them pulling at each other.

Tina watched them and sighed. 'We won't be like them, will we, Trevor?'

Uh-oh! Alarm bells ringing again! I edged further from her.

'No, we won't,' I said heavily. 'We won't be at all like them in any way whatsoever.'

Tina smiled. 'I knew that. You couldn't be like Charlie, ever!' And she moved towards me.

Noooo! I hastily glanced at Kriss's stopwatch and leaped to my feet. 'Kriss has been gone for more than nine minutes! Where is he? What's happened to him?'

We looked all around but there was no sign at all.

'Maybe he's been kidnapped,' Tina suggested.

The watch carried on ticking. Ten minutes passed, and still no sign. Eleven. This was getting ridiculous. Where could he be?

We heard barking in the woods. There was a loud squawking and clattering noise and suddenly ten pheasants came bursting out from the trees and struggled into the air, still blathering at each other like a bunch of angry kids from nursery.

Then Streaker appeared, towing Kriss behind. The runner was covered in bits of grass and twigs, branches, leaves and sweat. He had several scratches on his arms and legs. He looked absolutely exhausted. I stopped the watch.

'Twelve minutes, forty-eight seconds,' I told him. It was a disaster.

Kriss just stood there,
bent double, hands on
knees, panting and panting.

'Dog,' he gasped.
'That dog! Dragged me
everywhere! (Gasp!) Chased
rabbits. Chased birds. (Pant-
pant!) Chased squirrels,
butterflies, litter. (Gasp!)
She even chased ME! Never
again! Never!'

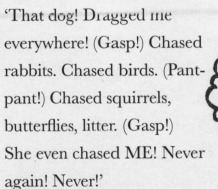

Kriss looked at us with wild eyes, straightened up and limped away down the path. 'Never again!' he called back, before finally disappearing round a bend.

Tina and I looked at each other and then at Streaker. She sat there in her angelic pose, with her tongue hanging out.

'So,' Tina said slowly. 'Not exactly a success then.'

4. The Lucky Running-shorts

The next day arrived and Tina and I were still puzzling over how to help Kriss speed up. We decided to go back to the woods to see how he was getting on. We took the frisbee with us in case it was a while before Kriss turned up for training.

I was rapidly going off the idea of Streaker ever skateboarding, but I could easily picture her winning gold for the frisbee event. She was a natural runner and jumper. I once watched Streaker snatch a beefburger from a man just as he was about to put it into his mouth! With a bound and a leap she'd sailed through the air. Was it a bird? Was it a plane? No, it was SuperStreak – the burger-burglar!

I turned to Tina. 'I've just thought of another

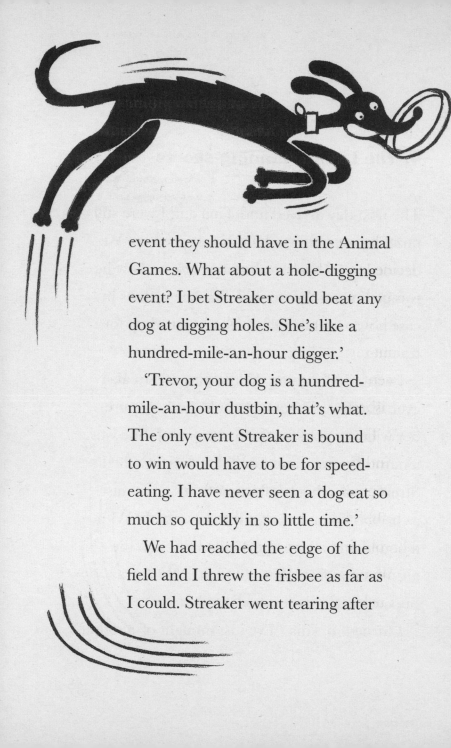

event they should have in the Animal
Games. What about a hole-digging
event? I bet Streaker could beat any
dog at digging holes. She's like a
hundred-mile-an-hour digger.'

'Trevor, your dog is a hundred-
mile-an-hour dustbin, that's what.
The only event Streaker is bound
to win would have to be for speed-
eating. I have never seen a dog eat so
much so quickly in so little time.'

We had reached the edge of the
field and I threw the frisbee as far as
I could. Streaker went tearing after

it, bouncing through the long grass. As
the frisbee came sailing back to earth
she leaped up and CLUNK! She'd got
it! She came racing back to us. I held
out my hand to her in triumph. Streaker
went zooming straight past with the
frisbee still in her mouth.

Tina cried out. 'She's seen a rabbit!'
And she had. That daft dog of mine
went all over the place, with the
rabbit bouncing ahead and the frisbee
wobbling about in her mouth like a
dinner plate waiting for its dinner.
Luckily it was a dinner that never

arrived because the rabbit suddenly disappeared down a tiny hole where a dog couldn't follow – not even a slinky-thin one like Streaker.

We were so busy laughing at her that we didn't see Charlie Smugg until we were almost on top of him. It seemed that he'd been watching us. Then I noticed his three Alsatians prowling in the grass some way behind.

'I suppose you think your dog's clever, catching that frisbee thing,' he sneered. 'I bet you my dogs can do better than that.'

'Your Alsatians?' I gulped. 'Streaker's a lot better than them.'

'No way,' snarled Charlie. 'I bet you my dog can beat yours any day.'

Tina shook her head. 'We don't do bets. But I can tell you that Streaker can beat any one of your Alsatians.'

'OK, clever-clogs. Is that a challenge?' Charlie had an evil smirk on his face. Why hadn't I guessed he had some kind of trick up his sleeve?

'Yes, it's a challenge,' Tina said proudly.

'Tina!' I hissed. 'Streaker's MY dog!' But she didn't take any notice, and Charlie smirked even more.

'OK then. Here's the deal. You put your dog in the Animal Games frisbee event, and I'll put in my Alsatians. Then we'll see who's left with egg on their face. So that means not only will your stupid mutt lose the running race to Lamborghini, but she'll also lose to my Alsatians in the frisbee event. Oh – don't think I mentioned it before, but my Alsatians did a frisbee event last year. I trained 'em for months. They won by miles. You're going to lose, lover-boy, and there'll be nobody to kiss you better except your GIRLFRIEND! Hurr hurr hurrr!' And he sloped off, making kissy noises to the air.

I stuck my hands in my pockets, kicked the ground and looked daggers at Tina.

'You've got us into a right mess,' I complained.

'I couldn't help it. Charlie is such a fat big-head. Anyhow, he's not going to win – we are. Streaker is the best frisbee catcher in the world.'

I don't know if Streaker understood Tina, but she went off and celebrated by rolling in something EXTREMELY SMELLY AND NASTY.

When we got to the woods, we discovered we weren't the only people there. An elderly couple was sitting on a rug with a pizza-picnic, almost exactly where Tina and I had sat the previous day. They gave us a cheerful wave.

'Who are they?'

'How should I know?' said Tina. 'Maybe they're Kriss's parents.'

We wandered across and smiled at them.

'We're watching young Kriss,' beamed the man.

'We're his fan club,' said his wife with a little laugh.

'Are you his mum and dad?' asked Tina, and the woman burst out laughing.

'No, no, no, dearie. I'm Mrs Akani and –' she gestured at her husband – 'Mr Akani. We like watching Kriss train.'

'Do you think he'll get gold at the Games?' I asked hopefully.

'Who knows?' said Mr Akani. 'He's fast, but so is Azi Numa, I think.'

'Kriss is trying to get faster,' I told them.

Mrs Akani patted the ground next to her. 'Sit down, have some pizza,' she said. 'I'm afraid the base is a bit thick. I was busy and my husband made them. What can you do?' Mrs Akani glanced fondly at her husband and they both chuckled.

'If you don't like my pizzas,' Mr Akani said to his wife, 'don't eat them!' And they started laughing again. What a jolly couple.

At that moment Streaker started barking and jumping up and down. A moment later Kriss Okonjo himself appeared from the woods, stopped and looked at his watch. He shook his head. I called out to him.

'No better?'

Kriss looked up and saw us – and he saw Streaker too. 'It's a lot better than when she was helping me yesterday,' he said flatly. He came over and explained to Mr and Mrs Akani what had happened the previous day with the dog.

'What? This dog here?' asked Mrs Akani. 'But she looks so harmless.'

'She is harmless,' I told her. 'It's just that somehow she manages to muck things up for everyone.'

Right on cue, Streaker began racing round and round Kriss's legs in ever-smaller circles until eventually she jumped up and knocked him flying. Poor Kriss! He went tumbling backwards and sat down with a **WHUMP!!** on the picnic rug, right on one of Mr Akani's mini-pizzas.

Kriss leaped up at once, wiping his backside angrily. 'These are my best running shorts, my lucky running shorts! Look what your pesky dog has done now!'

But there was no time to say any more because Streaker was after the pizza that was still stuck to Kriss's bottom! Kriss tried to back off, but Streaker was after him.

Kriss turned tail and fled. All at once he was in a running race with a dog! She was hot on his heels, snapping at his rear, while Kriss ran to save his life – or at least save his bottom!

'Aaaargh!' screamed Kriss as he disappeared into the woods, and both the international runner and the international doggy nuisance disappeared from sight.

5. How to Catch a Frisbee, or Not

'Streaker!' I yelled, leaping to my feet. Did she take any notice? Of course not.

'Oh dear,' murmured Mr Akani, and we all stared in horror at the silent woods, imagining the kind of headlines that would appear in the next day's newspapers.

INTERNATIONAL ATHLETE HAS BOTTOM EATEN BY DOG! FORCED TO RETIRE FROM INTERNATIONAL GAMES

The silence was broken by another scream as Kriss burst out from the woods with Streaker still in hot pursuit. He came hurtling straight towards us.

'Heeeeeelp! Get this dog off me!'

As Kriss flashed past I threw myself with all my strength on Streaker and managed to bring her down. We rolled into the long grass while Kriss collapsed on the ground, panting heavily.

'I've never run so fast,' he complained. 'That dog . . . that dog should be locked up. First she drags me through every hedge for miles around and then she tries to eat my – my you-know-what.'

'Sorry,' I muttered.

Mr Akani turned to Kriss. 'Mr Okonjo –'

'Kriss, please. Call me Kriss.'

Mr Akani bowed his head briefly. 'Kriss, I understand you are trying to improve your time?'

'I am, but I seem to be hitting an invisible wall. I just can't get any faster.'

'Then maybe you should let my wife help you,' suggested Mr Akani.

We all looked at Mrs Akani. She didn't look like someone who could train international runners. I have no idea what an athletics trainer should look like, but I'm pretty sure they wouldn't look like Mrs Akani, who was more of a – well, *waddly* kind of person. I don't mean that unkindly, but Mrs Akani was pretty large – and round, with short legs and short arms. Besides, she looked at least fifty, maybe sixty, which is pretty old if you ask me.

I think Kriss felt the same way. His eyebrows went up a bit, but he was very polite and asked Mrs Akani just how she thought she could help.

'I'm sure you know all there is to know about running, Kriss, and I know nothing. But, my dear, you just told us you felt as if you were hitting a wall trying to get faster. That wall has nothing to do with speed. That wall is something in your mind.'

Tina and Kriss and I were all agog to hear

more. This woman sounded as if she knew something useful.

'Barriers in your mind can seem very big and scary, not to mention impossible to break down. And yet it is only your mind that makes them so scary.'

'I can understand that,' Kriss said, nodding. 'But what can be done about it?'

'I am a hypnotist,' Mrs Akani declared. 'I have helped smokers give up smoking. I help people break down the barriers in their mind and overcome whatever problem they have. A woman came to me last month and told me she was so afraid of spiders she wouldn't go in her own bathroom until her husband had checked it over for spiders from top to bottom. I hypnotized her and told her she was no longer afraid. Now she has no problem with spiders. In fact she has just bought one as a pet.'

Kriss leaned forward and took Mrs Akani's hand. 'Do you think you can help me break down my barrier, so I can run faster?'

It was Mr Akani who answered that question. 'Put it this way, Mr Okonjo. It can't do you any harm. If it fails, you will still be running just as you are today. But if it succeeds you will be faster.'

'And I would be honoured to treat you,' Mrs Akani announced. 'And there will be no charge for my services. If you win gold – that will be my reward!'

'How long will it take for the hypnotism to work?' asked Kriss. 'There are only a few days left before I have to join the athletes at the official Training Camp and then it will be the International Games.'

Mrs Akani sat back and thought. 'It might take a few days. It depends on how strong the wall in your mind is. But it is worth a try.'

Kriss flashed a huge smile at us. 'I can tell this

is going to work!' he announced. 'This is the best thing that could have happened. Thank you, Mrs Akani!' Kriss held Streaker's head and waggled it with his hands, making her ears flap about. 'As for you, Streaker, I think Mrs Akani needs to hypnotize you and PUT a barrier in your doggy mind to stop you causing so much trouble!'

The three of them went off together so that Kriss could have his first hypnotism session. As for Tina and me, we had our own work to get on with — training Streaker for the frisbee competition.

Unfortunately, Streaker had more or less eaten my frisbee, but Tina had brought hers along. Streaker was bouncing up and down on her lead, almost yanking my arm off, so I set her free and WHOOOOOOSH! She was off. Honestly, that dog is a rocket on legs. I didn't bother to call her back because I knew she wouldn't come. We would just have to wait until she had run off some of her amazing energy.

We sat down on the grass. Tina lay back and stared up at the clouds.

'There's a frog,' she said, pointing at the sky.

'It looks a bit squashed to me,' I said, lying down as well.

'No it isn't. It's crouching down.'

'Looks like it's been run over by a truck,' I muttered. Tina dug her elbow into my side.

'It's a frog and it's sitting up now.'

I was sitting up too, holding my side. 'That hurt.'

'There, there, poor Trevvy-wevvy. Shall I kiss it better?'

I was on my feet in an instant. 'I wonder where

Streaker's got to,' I said, hastily changing the subject. 'Streaker! STREAKER!'

Amazingly, the dog came bounding back, two ears and a tongue all happily flapping away.

'Time for some frisbee-catching, Streaker,' I said. I showed her the frisbee and she sniffed it all over. She even licked it.

'She's going to love this,' I told Tina. I drew back my arm. 'Ready, Streaker? Get ready! One, two, three –!'

The frisbee went skimming off through the air and Streaker went – well, actually she didn't 'went' at all. In fact she sat down and looked at me. She looked at my empty hand as if to say – '*Where did that thing go?*'

Tina smiled. 'She enjoyed that, didn't she?'

'She just needs to get the hang of it, that's all. She did it recently, you saw her.'

'I know. But now she has to do it at the Animal Games or Charlie Smugg will be boasting about it for weeks.'

Tina was right. I stomped off through the grass, fetched the frisbee and shoved it under Streaker's nose. 'This time you have to run after it and catch it, OK?'

Streaker was looking at me with shiny eyes. She was the picture of – I would like to say the picture of intelligence, but in fact she looked about as intelligent as an ice cream.

I waved the frisbee at her once more. 'Ready? One, two, three –'

Swooooosh!

'She's after it!' cried Tina. 'Go, Streaker, go!'

The frisbee was sailing through the air, slowly skimming down towards the ground. Streaker was galloping after it with great big strides.

'That's it, Streaker!' I yelled after her. 'Catch it!'

The frisbee was coming down . . . Streaker was almost on it . . . the frisbee was clipping the grass!

Streaker shot past, running and running, and behind her the frisbee bumped on to the ground while Streaker went tearing ahead, full of the joys of running. She didn't stop until she reached the far end of the field, and went crashing into the hedge. She'd never been much good at braking.

By that time I had collected the frisbee and trudged back to Tina. I collapsed on the grass and we waited for the dog to come back.

'Charlie Smugg is going to laugh his head off. He'll never let us live this down.'

'Trevor, this is the first practice. We've got a few more days before the big event. We'll work something out. We always do.'

'Yeah,' I muttered darkly. 'We could go and find a dog THAT ACTUALLY DOES WHAT YOU WANT IT TO DO!' I suddenly yelled, getting back to my feet as I spotted Streaker returning. 'Look, you manky mutt! This is a frisbee. Fetch the frisbee! FETCH!'

Tina calmly took the frisbee from me. 'Let me do it. It never works if you shout. People don't like being shouted at and neither do animals. Stay calm, OK? I'll throw it. Here we go, Streaker. Ready?'

Tina launched the frisbee. It lifted into the air, soaring on the wind. Streaker went leaping through the grass, right beneath it, going 'woof, woof, woof!' as if to say 'I'm coming to get you!'

'She's going to do it, she's going to do it!' Tina whispered excitedly, as the frisbee carried on sailing above the grass. Streaker followed, ears flapping wildly, glancing up from time to time, and then, and then –

Streaker suddenly halted, scratched behind her left ear, crouched down and had a long, long TIDDLE. In the distance the frisbee glided down and landed.

'Well I certainly didn't expect that,' Tina sighed.

6. More Competition

We saw Kriss Okonjo again today. He was with Mr and Mrs Akani, up near the woods. Tina and I had gone back to the field for you-know-what. (Frisbee practice!) We asked them how the first hypnotism session had gone. Mrs Akani smiled.

'It was fine. Kriss is a good student.'

The runner laughed. 'It's funny to think of myself as a student. It's seven years since I was in school.' He put a hand on Mrs Akani's shoulder – Kriss must be at least half a metre taller than her! 'I felt good after that session, you know, relaxed and well rested.'

Mrs Akani nodded. 'That is how it should be. Now you can concentrate better on your running. Here, give me your watch and I shall time you.'

Kriss handed over his watch and I set mine

to zero. He did a few exercises, stretching his muscles, and then he was off.

'Just look at him,' said Mr Akani, shaking his head. 'That lad runs like a gazelle.'

It was true. Kriss made running look so easy.

'It's those long legs,' murmured Tina. 'I'd like legs like those.'

'You'd look pretty silly with black legs and white arms,' I sniggered.

'And you'd look pretty silly with a black eye and white face,' Tina snapped back.

Mr Akani grinned at me.

We waited by the woods for Kriss to complete his course. Tina told the Akanis about the Sports Day they had held at school and how she'd got gold for the high jump. They asked me if I'd got anything and I said, yes, a virus, and they all laughed. It wasn't funny to me. I would rather have been at school taking part than lying in bed feeling sorry for myself.

'Here he comes,' said Mr Akani. 'Get ready with the watch, Miriam.'

Mrs Akani pressed the stop button. 'Eight minutes, five point nine one seconds,' she read out, setting it back to zero.

A huge beam spread across Kriss's face. I blinked several times and shook my watch. 'That's odd,' I murmured. 'Mine says eight minutes eight point three.'

Kriss's face fell, but Mr Akani took my wrist and looked at my watch. He smiled.

'I don't want to upset you, lad, but your watch

is not really up to scratch. Look at Kriss's here.
This is a very expensive piece of machinery.'

Kriss nodded. 'It has to
be. I paid a lot of money
for that. It's super-
accurate.'

I gave a grunt.
'Yeah. I guess
so. Wish I had one like yours! It's got so many
buttons. What's that one for?'

'Different time zones,' Kriss answered.

'And this one?'

'Altimeter – tells you how high you are,
anywhere in the world.'

'And that one?'

'Not sure. I think it does the washing up.'

We burst out laughing while Kriss looked a bit
embarrassed. 'To tell you the truth, I haven't a
clue what that one does, but I've got a booklet
back home that tells you. It's about a hundred
pages long.'

Kriss gazed over our heads and back at his training ground. 'Eight minutes five point nine. That's faster than the record – and definitely faster than Azi Numa. Thanks, Mrs Akani.'

'We're not done yet, Kriss,' she beamed. 'We need to get you faster still and make sure you nail that gold right on the head.'

She turned to us. 'We'll leave you to your training session now. Good luck with that frisbee and maybe we'll see you another day.'

The three of them went off together, and Tina and I moved higher into the field so the frisbee could get a good flight.

'Trust Mum and Dad to buy me a cheap watch for my birthday,' I complained.

'Your watch is fine, Trevor. You're ten. You can hardly expect your parents to buy you a watch like Kriss's. It was pretty spectacular.'

Sometimes Tina talks quite a lot of sense. She was right, of course. Still, I can't wait until I'm Kriss's age. Then I'll buy a watch that can

do everything – including the washing up AND
tidying my bedroom!

We were about to throw the frisbee for
Streaker when three figures appeared on the
path. I knew at once Charlie Smugg wasn't one
of them because they were all about my size. It
didn't take long for me to recognize them either.
It was three kids from school – Sophie, Tim and
Nicky, and they were all carrying frisbees. I like
Sophie.

'Hi!' she called.

'Why is she with them?' Tina hissed at me. I
looked at her, puzzled.

'Why shouldn't she be with them?'

Tina kicked at the grass. All of a sudden she
seemed cross, heaven knows why.

'Are you practising for the frisbee
competition?' asked Nicky.

'Maybe,' I answered.

'Thought so. Charlie Smugg told us you were
having a competition with him so we asked if

we could join in, and he said no problem. It's a great idea.'

Tina and I looked at the collection of dogs they had with them.

Sophie had a dachshund – you know, a sausage dog. Tim had a collie.

'What kind of dog is that?' asked Sophie, pointing at Streaker.

'I knew she was trouble,' Tina said to me, under her breath.

'Streaker? Well, she's kind of everything.'

'Like a pizza,' laughed Sophie. 'You should call her Pizza!'

'See,' Tina hissed again. 'Trouble.'

I reddened. 'Actually, she's called Streaker because she's like a streak of lightning. She can run really fast.'

'Looks like she's got a bit of greyhound blood in her,' Nicky observed, and I nodded.

'Yep. She's half greyhound.'

'And the other half is ham and pineapple! Pizza!' Tim declared.

'She'll beat your collie any day,' I said quietly, and he shut up, because he knew it was true.

'Are you up here to train?' asked Sophie, and Tina nodded.

'But we've just finished,' I said quickly. There was no way I wanted them to see how useless Streaker was at catching a frisbee. 'Do you mind if we watch you?'

Sophie shrugged and took her dog off the lead.

'She's called Trudi. Come on, Trudi. Are you ready?'

The dachshund fretted around the frisbee and then Sophie threw it. Off it went, and Trudi went charging after it, diving into the grass like a submarine on legs. All we could see was the grass waving here and there, with a lot of barking. The frisbee sailed across the field and landed. Trudi was still running round in circles about three metres away from us.

Tina and I howled with laughter. It was pretty funny, after all. Sophie stared at us with a face like concrete.

'She couldn't see it. The grass is too long.'

'I know,' Tina hiccuped, holding her sides. 'It was very funny.'

Then Tim had a trial with his collie, Chips.
First he prepared the dog.

'Sit. Stay,' Tim ordered quietly, and at each
command the dog obeyed. My heart sank. This
dog had been TRAINED! It was something I'd
been trying to do with Streaker for YEARS –
without success.

'Go!' Tim cried, as he launched the frisbee.
Chips went leaping and bounding
through the grass, following the
path of the frisbee exactly,
and as it neared the grass
– LEAP! Chips rose
in the air and
– SNAP!

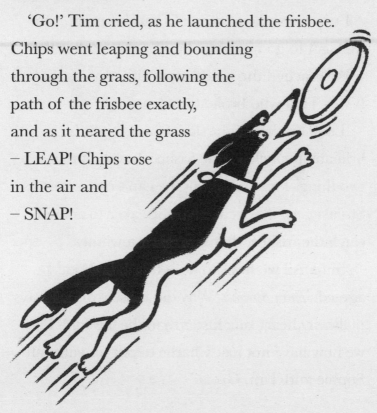

He clamped his jaws round the frisbee and came trotting back with it safely in his mouth.

'Sit,' ordered Tim, and Chips sat down while Tim quietly took the frisbee from the dog's mouth.

Sophie clapped. 'Brilliant, Tim! Oh, Chips, you're so clever. Clever, clever, clever dog!'

Tina leaned close to me. 'I hate her.'

I tried to smile at them. 'That was good. Oh well, got to go now. Maybe see you another time.'

We reached the road before either of us spoke. It was Tina who broke the silence.

'Look on the bright side. Chips might be brilliant at catching the frisbee, but we know two things for sure. Firstly, he can't run as fast as Streaker, so, if we can train Streaker to actually catch the frisbee, then we've got a winner.'

'Sure. All we have to do is train Streaker,' I agreed. *Train Streaker.* Why did those words always make my heart sink faster than the *Titanic*? 'Plus, we now have not just Charlie to put up with but Sophie and Tim. Great.'

'And secondly,' Tina continued, ignoring my grumps, 'Chips is pretty good, as we have just seen. He might well be fast enough to beat Charlie's Alsatians, in which case he won't win, which is what he wants to do, so he will be very disappointed.'

I thought about this. Once again Tina was right. It cheered me up a bit, but I do wish she'd stop being right so often.

7. Pizzas Are a Good Idea

I woke in the night with a brilliant idea. It was so good I sat right up in bed and told my teddy. OK, I know, I know; you're thinking *Trevor's ten and he's got a teddy! Ha ha ha ha!*

Well, just so that you know – I HAVE NOT GOT A TEDDY, OK?!!

I used to have a teddy, like most children, when I was small, and that teddy still happens to be in my bedroom. He sits on my bookshelf, which happens to be on the wall at the end of my bed. So when I sit up in bed I just happen to see my teddy sometimes. OK?

Anyhow – my brilliant idea, in one word – pizzas. My brain was saying to me: *Streaker likes food – a lot. In fact she's a greedy guzzler. Pizzas are food. Pizzas are like frisbees. Throw pizzas instead of*

frisbees and Streaker will run after them.

Was that a brilliant idea, or not? It certainly
was, so I put my head on the pillow and went
back to sleep with a very big smile on my face,
and the smile was still there when I woke up next
morning. I went straight off to tell Tina. (Well
actually I got dressed first, of course, ha ha!) Tina
was impressed. (With my idea that is, not because
I'd got dressed.)

'That's great,' she said. 'Just one problem. When you throw the pizza, won't most of the food fall off?'

I shook my head. 'Nah. Maybe a little, the odd bit of tomato or something.'

'Hmmm. Just another problem,' Tina went on, holding up a finger. 'Won't the pizza be all floppy and not fly very well?'

'Nah. It'll be fine,' I muttered. I was getting a bit fed up with my friend.

'Hmmm. And just another little problem,' she went on relentlessly. 'Won't it fall to bits when you try to throw it?'

I fixed Tina with my deadly stare. 'I thought you said it was a great idea,' I reminded her.

'It IS a great idea,' she said. 'It's what happens when you actually put your ideas into practice that bothers me.'

OK, I'd had enough. 'Fine,' I snapped. 'I'll try it out and let you know how it goes.'

Tina's eyes widened. 'You don't want me to come and help?'

'NO! I can do it on my own. See you later. Maybe.'

That showed her. I went stomping back to my house. We've nearly always got pizzas in our house – in the freezer, the fridge, the oven, on plates or in our mouths. My favourite is salami, mozzarella and tomato. I peered into the fridge and I was in luck. There was a whole cooked pizza, sitting on the middle shelf.

I eyed it thoughtfully. If I took it, Mum would certainly miss it. What if I replaced it with a frozen one? With a bit of luck it would defrost before Mum came to the fridge and she'd open the door and find a pizza. The only difference would be that it wasn't cooked. So she'd probably think she must have forgotten to cook it, because there it was, waiting for her. Mum's always forgetting things.

I listened out for problems. Dad was out playing golf and I could hear Mum on her rowing machine. (She hasn't fallen off that one yet, but I expect she will. She'll probably drown.) I zipped over to the freezer, grabbed a pizza, unwrapped it, took the cooked pizza off its plate, put the frozen one there instead and popped the cooked one carefully into a plastic bag.

Streaker was watching all this with great interest, following every move the pizza made, right into the bag. Now she was trotting after the bag as I headed for the front door.

'Just taking Streaker for a walk,' I shouted.

'OK!' Mum answered, and in no time I was out of the door and heading up the road.

Once we reached the field I let Streaker off her lead. Normally when I do this she immediately goes zooming off at hyperspeed in a dizzying blur of legs and I don't see her again for half an hour or so. But she had her nose glued to the plastic bag and was not going anywhere until she knew what was going to happen to that pizza.

I pulled it from the bag as carefully as I could but, even so, several bits dropped off, which was annoying but hardly my fault as I was struggling to keep the pizza out of Streaker's jaws. She was barking around my legs, trying to climb up me and generally getting overexcited, especially when the bits of food fell off.

The pizza was also a bit floppy. If it had just come out of the oven it would have been stiff and crispy, but it had come out of the fridge, so it was cold, clammy and floppy. I held it as best I could. I already had a sinking feeling that I wouldn't be able to throw it very far.

'OK. Streaker, get ready. This is it. Test flight,

number one.' I drew back my arm and flung
the pizza into the air. I think it must have flown
a good three CENTIMETRES before it fell to
pieces and most of it landed on my feet. I was
left holding a small, soggy bit of crust that had
broken off when I tried to launch it. Streaker
very kindly leaped up and gobbled it down, along
with my fingers.

'Ow! Streaker! Do you mind!'

I put her back on the lead and trudged home. I was fed up, mostly because it had happened just like Tina had said it would. I could hear her voice ringing in my ears. '*The food will fall off . . . it will be all floppy . . . it will fall to bits.*' She is such a know-all.

I was determined to show her up. I knew my brainwave had been a good one. There must be some way to make it work. I now knew that floppy, cold pizzas wouldn't fly, so that left me with two choices.

1. Get a crispy pizza straight from the oven. Problem: almost impossible to achieve. Plus it would be too hot coming straight from the oven AND by the time I got it up to the field it would be too cold and all floppy again.

2. Use a frozen, uncooked pizza. Problem: would Streaker fancy it?

I plumped for choice number two. Maybe it would work. There was only one way to find out.

There were plenty of frozen pizzas in the freezer – well, four at any rate. Mum was still rowing in the front room. She'd been at it for ages. She must have been halfway across the Atlantic by now. Dad was still out with his golfing buddies. Slipping a frozen pizza up my jumper was easy-peasy. (I couldn't find a plastic bag.)

Streaker was getting confused. She kept looking at me, wondering why we were going back up the road we'd only just come down. I think she was also wondering why I was walking in such an odd way, sucking in my chest, trying to avoid contact with an ice-cold, rock-hard pizza. My shirt was getting damp and clammy. I honestly thought I might be the first person in history to get frostbite on their tummy.

As soon as we stepped into the field, I pulled

out the pizza and gave my stomach a good rub
to warm it up. Streaker didn't seem to be the
least bit interested and spent more time looking
at the fluffy clouds in the sky than the pizza.
I shoved it right under her nose. She sniffed
it once, shook her ears and wandered off to
examine a dandelion.

I waited five minutes and let the sun melt
the glaze of ice on the top of the pizza so at
least she could see bits of cheese and salami. It
seemed I'd picked my favourite pizza, which was
a shame, but I couldn't go back and change it.
I showed Streaker the pizza again and this time
she was a bit more interested, so I threw it.

Streaker went charging after it. Unfortunately,
pizzas don't fly as gracefully as frisbees.
Mine went slicing through the air for a few
metres, wobbled, tipped to one side, went
into a nosedive and crash-landed. Streaker
immediately clamped her teeth round it,
expecting to get a nice juicy chunk of pizza

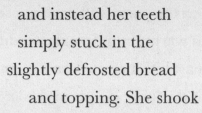

and instead her teeth simply stuck in the slightly defrosted bread and topping. She shook her head from side to side, trying to dislodge it, but her teeth were firmly glued. She looked as if she had a dinner plate stuck in her mouth and carried on shaking her head, again and again, and growling. I managed to grab hold of her and after a bit of levering and twisting she got her top jaw free and then the bottom. I looked at the pizza. It had teeth holes right the way through and a lot of dog-slobber. Lovely!

I tried throwing it once more and this time the pizza skimmed a lot further. Streaker went bouncing after it and managed to get it just as it landed. Things were looking up, but the pizza was defrosting. I gave it one more try. Streaker

actually jumped into the air, trying to snatch
it, but again the pizza landed first. This time
Streaker ate it. So she'd now had two pizzas, but
at least she was getting the idea.

I was about to head back home when the
Akanis arrived, along with Kriss. They waved
and I went over.

'We're going for gold,' grinned Kriss as he
did his warm-up exercises. 'I've had another
hypnosis session. I'm sure I'm going to run fast
today. That's good, because the race is the day
after tomorrow. This evening I join the whole
team at the training camp, and once I'm there I
shan't be able to speak to anyone apart from my
teammates. It will be nothing but training until
the great day. OK, I'm all ready.'

Kriss handed his watch to Mrs Akani. I set
mine to zero too. Maybe it would keep better
time today. Kriss set off and we sat down to wait.

'Your dog – is she all right?' asked Mr Akani.
'She looks a bit off colour.'

Streaker was moping about, her head low down, her ears all droopy. She swallowed and gulped several times and then ***SPLURRGGG!*** She threw up right in front of Mr Akani.

'Sorry,' I murmured, but there was nothing I could do about it. We moved away to a more pleasant spot and I got into conversation with

Mrs Akani about hypnosis. She explained that it was dangerous to try if you didn't know what you were doing. 'You can do more harm than good,' she said.

We soon spotted Kriss on his way out of the woods and got ready with our watches. Mrs Akani punched the air.

'Well done, Kriss! Eight minutes, five point one. That's almost a second faster than yesterday. Now, don't forget, last hypnosis session tonight at seven o'clock.'

I didn't even bother to tell them what my watch said. (Eight minutes, ten point two! Which was WORSE than yesterday!) I gazed enviously at Kriss's fab watch. Still, it was good that he was getting faster.

We walked towards home together. Kriss had left his car nearby and drove off, but I saw the Akanis to the end of their road, which was near mine, and waved goodbye as they went into their house.

As soon as I reached home, Mum came out of the kitchen. (She'd obviously managed to find her way back to shore.)

'Trevor,' she said, in a tone of voice that instantly put me on red alert. 'What can you tell me about missing pizzas?'

UH-OH!

8. Trevor and Tina Fall Off the Sofa

I'm still alive. I know, it's a miracle. How did I escape Death? I told Mum the truth, sort of.

'Streaker ate it. I left the fridge door open for a few seconds and, the next thing, she'd eaten it.' (Which she had, so that bit was true, and I reckoned it didn't really matter where or when she'd eaten the pizza. After all, nothing was going to bring the pizza back – unless you count Streaker throwing it up in the field. Urgh!)

'But how did she get it?' asked Mum, quite bewildered. 'It was on the middle shelf!'

'Mum,' I said, 'dogs can jump.'

'Let me get this straight, Trevor. Streaker jumped up and swiped the pizza off the plate?'

'Exactly,' I nodded.

'And after that she got a frozen pizza out of the

freezer and jumped up again and put the frozen pizza on the plate where the cooked one had been?' Mum raised both eyebrows. She'd got me there.

'Look, I didn't want her to get into trouble so I put the frozen one there. I was hoping you wouldn't notice. You're always forgetting things.'

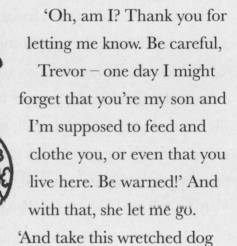

'Oh, am I? Thank you for letting me know. Be careful, Trevor – one day I might forget that you're my son and I'm supposed to feed and clothe you, or even that you live here. Be warned!' And with that, she let me go.

'And take this wretched dog with you!' she called after me.

So I survived. In fact I reckoned I'd got off pretty lightly. I took Streaker and went to Tina's to tell her the news.

'Kriss is getting faster and my watch is getting

slower. It's useless. I'm going to get a new one as soon as.'

'As soon as what?' asked Tina.

'Just as soon as,' I repeated. 'When I've got the money, obviously. Oh yes, other news just in,' I added so, SO casually, 'I tried the pizza-frisbee idea and it's starting to work.'

'Really? Truly? The pizza didn't fall to bits?'

I treated Tina to my biggest smile. 'I used a frozen pizza.'

'Frozen? Wow. Did Streaker like it?'

A picture of Streaker with her jaws firmly stuck in the half-frozen pizza came to mind. 'She couldn't keep her teeth out of it,' I said.

'Oh, that's good. And did she catch it?'

'That's the bit that still needs practice. I'm going to have another go tomorrow. Did you know that Kriss leaves for training camp tonight?'

'Let's wish him luck before he goes,' Tina suggested. 'Mum wants me to go into town and get some stuff for her. Are you coming?'

'I guess. Mum's a bit unpredictable at the moment so it's best if I keep clear of her.'

'What's up?' asked Tina.

'She discovered a pizza missing from the fridge and I had to tell her that Streaker had eaten it.'

'Trevor!'

'Where else did you expect me to get a pizza from?' But I was laughing. It had been pretty funny. Even the floppy frisbee had been funny, really, but there was no way I was going to let Tina know about that.

We wandered into town with both the dogs. It's quite useful when we have Mouse with us. He's so huge that everyone gets out of the way because he goes ahead, mowing a path through the crowd for us and we sail along behind him.

Unfortunately, it's almost impossible to sail round Charlie Smugg, especially when he's got Sharon Blenkinsop with him and they've got their arms interlinked. As soon as he saw us, Charlie started singing.

'Here comes the bride, all fat and wide –'

Which is a bit much coming from an over-

large, heavily-pimpled, baboon-eared, ugly-faced cabbage-brain like Charlie. 'How's the frisbee-catching going?' he sniggered.

'Pretty good,' I answered. 'How about your Alsatians?'

Charlie smirked. 'They don't need to practice. Got 'em well trained, you see. TRAINED,' he repeated loudly. 'That's not a word your dog understands really, is it?' he taunted. 'TRAINED?'

'Shall we get a drink from the cafe, Trev?' Tina suggested, ignoring Charlie completely.

'Good idea,' I growled.

Charlie chuckled. 'Yeah, you two luvvy-wuvvies go and get a drinky-poo. Then afterwards you can go and buy her a wedding ring! Hurr hurr hurr!'

Honestly, Charlie Smugg is about as funny as rice pudding. (In other words totally yuck.)

Charlie and the luvverly Sharon went sloping off, chortling and smirking. We collected the

shopping that Tina's mum wanted and went back
to her place.

I like Tina's house. It's quieter than ours. For
one thing, Tina's mum doesn't waste her life
constantly rowing or cycling round the front
room. We spent most of the time having a fairly
useless argument about dogs, frisbees and pizzas,
while Mouse and Streaker argued over Mouse's
favourite cushion. All I can say is that the cushion
had an awful lot of foam padding inside to start
with, but ended up with ALL the padding on
the outside by the time they had finished their
quarrel and Streaker had won.

Tina put the telly on. It was the news, which is usually utterly boring because it's always about grey people talking about money and houses and golf. However, today they were talking to some of the athletes taking part in the International Games.

'Kriss might be on it,' Tina said, so we sat and watched.

Kriss wasn't on it in fact, but someone else was – Azi Numa, Kriss's biggest rival. He was being interviewed by a reporter, Tamsin Plank.

'Do you think you can beat Kriss Okonjo?' she asked. He gave a wide grin.

'Of course! The race is mine!'

'There we have it,' Tamsin Plank said to camera. 'Azi Numa has thrown down the gauntlet. But let's hear from his fans. Earlier today I spoke to two of them.'

The camera swung round on to two elderly people.

MR AND MRS AKANI!

Were we surprised? I almost fell off the sofa.
Tina started to say something, but I clamped a
hand over her mouth so I could hear what was
going on. Tamsin Plank held up a microphone to
them.

'You believe that Azi is going to win this race,
don't you? Why is that?'

'He's the best runner,' said Mr Akani.

'He's the fastest on the planet,' Mrs Akani
added. 'I think he will take the record this time.'

Tamsin Plank smiled and glanced at the camera again. 'Of course, I should add that this couple are very special fans and they do have a particular interest in Azi because they are, in fact, his parents!'

And at that point I did fall off the sofa, and Tina fell off with me. We recovered just in time to hear Tamsin saying goodbye. 'Thank you, Mr and Mrs Numa, for joining us today, and that's all from Sports Round-Up. Back to the studio.'

Tina and I sat on the floor in silence for a few moments. My brain was in a whirl. Tina reached out, took hold of my hand and squeezed it.

'What are we going to do?' she whispered.

I looked deep into her eyes and spoke slowly and firmly. 'You're going to let go of my hand, thank you. That's what we're going to do.' And I quickly rescued it from her grasp.

9. Guess Who's on Television?

I thought hard, trying to get a grip on this startling piece of information that we had just heard. 'That was Mr and Mrs Akani, except they're not Mr and Mrs Akani, they're Mr and Mrs Numa, Azi Numa's parents.'

'Why do they call themselves Mr and Mrs Akani then?' Tina asked.

'Exactly. There's something weird going on and I don't like it.' I glanced at my watch. Seven o'clock. Kriss Okonjo was about to have his last session of hypnosis.

'Come on, we've got a bit of detective work to do,' I told Tina.

'Oh? That sounds fun.'

We set off without the dogs. I didn't want them getting in the way. Besides, you never knew what Streaker might do.

'Where are we going?' Tina asked, trying to keep up with me. I was almost running.

'The Akanis' house. I know where they live.'

'Are you planning to ask them why they call themselves Akani?'

'No. We're going to spy on them. I want to see what happens during hypnosis.'

'Why?' Tina was full of questions!

'Because I have an idea there's trickery going on, and if it turns out to be true then Kriss is in big trouble and he'll never win that gold medal. First of all, we have to check out the Akanis.'

'I suppose those people we saw on the telly might just happen to look like the Akanis,' Tina suggested.

'Both of them? A married couple turn up, and they both just happen to look like Mr and Mrs Akani? No – those people we saw were definitely the Akanis.'

We hurried on and turned into Marley Avenue.

I pointed out a small house on the end of a
terrace of four others. A narrow pathway went
down the side of the house to the back garden.
We walked past, trying hard to look inside the
front room without looking as if we were looking.

'We mustn't be spotted,' I whispered, crouching
down by the Akanis' front wall. I pulled Tina
down beside me. 'Keep your head low.'

I inched upwards and peered over the wall.
The Akanis' windows reflected light back at me.
It was useless. I couldn't see a thing. A loud voice
exploded in my ear and I almost jumped out of
my skin.

'Are you all right down there?'

'Argh! What?' I hastily looked up and found a large, young woman looming over me, frowning.

'I said, are you all right?' she boomed. 'You look as if you're in trouble. I'm a nurse, you know. Well, training to be a nurse. Exams next week. I could bandage you if you like.'

What on earth was she rabbiting on about? Why wouldn't she just go away? Tina and I lay on the pavement, gazing up at her.

'We're fine, thank you. We don't need bandaging.'

'How about I take your pulse? Wait a moment, I've got a whizzo electronic thermometer in my bag here. I could take your temperatures.'

'We're fine,' I repeated, keeping my voice as low as possible. The last thing we needed was some daft nurse attracting attention to us.

'No head wounds? No cuts or abrasions? Broken bones?' the nurse bellowed.

'No!' I hissed back.

'I know!' the nurse shouted. 'I bet one of you has diarrhoea – you know, runny tummy!'

'There's a boy up the road who's just been

sick,' Tina suggested. (Clever girl, Tina!)

I nodded hard. 'And I think there was blood too,'
I added.

'Really? My goodness. He might die,' said the
nurse. 'I'd better go and save him.'

'I think you better had,' I went on. 'He was up
the road and round the corner, near the newspaper
shop.'

'Don't worry!' cried the nurse-who-wasn't-quite-a-
nurse-yet. 'I'm on my way.' And she ran off making
a noise. 'Nee-naw, nee-naw, nee-naw!'

Tina looked at me. 'There isn't a newspaper shop
round the corner,' she said.

I grinned back at her. 'There isn't a boy up the
road either,' I reminded her and we did a quick high
five. 'Come on, let's try the back of the house.'

'Are you sure?'

'Yep.' I tried to sound very certain, and of course
I wasn't certain at all, and my heart was doing
somersaults, but we had to find out what was going
on.

We were in luck. All was quiet in the back garden, but there were voices coming from an open downstairs window. Tina and I crept up to it, still crouching down. I took a quick peek.

Mrs Akani-Numa was sitting opposite Kriss. His eyes were closed and Mrs Akani-Numa was talking to him in a low, dreamy voice.

'You are feeling sleepy. You are so tired. Your legs feel heavy, like lead. You can hardly run. You are so tired. You just want to lie down and go to sleep, go to sleep, go to sleep.' Mrs Akani-Numa paused and then gently asked Kriss how he felt.

'I must sleep,' he droned in a voice that seemed to come from Zombie-Land. 'I must sleep. I am so tired. No more running. I must sleep.'

Mrs Akani-Numa smiled to herself. 'Good,' she said. 'That is very good. Now then, when I snap my fingers you will wake up. You will remember nothing of this. You will be thinking, *now I can run really fast.* But on the day of the race all you will do is want to sleep. Ha ha!'

Mrs Akani-Numa snapped her fingers and Kriss woke with a start. He beamed at her.

I dropped back down to my knees. 'Let's get out of here. We've got to think what to do next.'

We slunk away and went to Tina's house. We sat on the edge of her bed for ages, kicking our heels and wondering what to do. The whole thing was mad. We talked about telling Tina's mum or my parents, but I shook my head.

'You know what they're like. They won't believe us. We don't have any proof. It's our word against theirs. If we tell the police, they'll question Kriss and he'll just say what he's been hypnotized to say. It feels like we're trapped.'

'We've got to tell Kriss,' Tina insisted. 'We must warn him.'

'Yeah. We can try that, I suppose. Do you know where he lives?'

Tina shook her head. 'There must be some way of contacting him.'

We sat in silence for a couple of minutes. 'Thought of anything?' I asked eventually, and she shook her head again. We felt so useless! It was driving me crazy.

'The only thing I can think of,' I ventured, 'is to Google his name and see if it comes up with any leads.'

Tina pulled across her laptop. Sometimes I'm quite envious of Tina. I haven't got a laptop, but she has. I've got a dad, though, and she hasn't. I'd swap my dad for a laptop any day! (No, not really! But you know what I mean!)

We Googled 'Kriss Okonjo' and up came a

pile of information about his trophies and races, and there was the name of the running club he belonged to and a telephone number for the club.

'We'll try that,' I said. 'It's the only chance we've got.'

Tina passed her mobile to me. A man answered. We asked if it was possible to speak to Kriss Okonjo.

'He's not here,' said the man.

'Can you give us a phone number for him? It's very important,' I said.

'Like I said, he's not here,' the man repeated.

'He's not here for anyone. Nobody can ring him. Kriss left early for the training camp. He's gone and we're not allowed to contact him now until all his races are finished. Nobody can contact him. Goodbye.'

The phone went dead. Tina and I looked at each other. This was getting worse and worse.

10. Another Brilliant Plan – Possibly

I hardly slept at all that night. A thousand and
one ideas were going through my head. There
must be something we could do, but I couldn't
think of anything. By the time morning came
I was at my wit's end. There was one day to go
before Kriss's race.

At breakfast I tried telling Mum and Dad
about the plot to slow Kriss down.

'Trevor, you must have dreamed all this in the
night,' said Mum.

'It's true.'

Dad folded his newspaper and chuckled.
'People don't do things like that. Hypnotize a
world-class athlete? That's the sort of rubbish you
read about in stories.'

'It's true,' I repeated. 'Tina and I went to their

house. We heard what Mrs Akani was saying.'

'You *think* you heard,' corrected Dad. 'I know
what you and Tina are like. You're always
hearing things.'

I stared at my dad. I was *always hearing things*?
What on earth was he on about?

'Dad –' I started, but he interrupted, waving
his paper at me as if I was a fly to be swatted.

'I don't want to hear any more about it. Go and play with your girlfriend or do something useful.'

Grrrrrrrrr! I clenched my teeth and stamped out of the house. *Go and play with your girlfriend.* I knew Dad thought he was being funny, but he was no better than Charlie Smugg, if you ask me. Anyhow, I took him at his word and went off to Tina's house.

She suggested we should go to the police, so we did. You can probably guess who was behind the desk – Sergeant Smugg – Charlie's dad.

'Oh. It's you two troublemakers,' he growled, so I knew we weren't going to get anywhere even before we had started. But we had to try.

Between us we unfolded our story. Sergeant Smugg stood behind the desk resting his head on one hand and looking utterly bored. He even yawned loudly several times. That's how much attention he gave us. When we finished, he gave a tired sigh.

'I happen to know Mr and Mrs Akani. Mrs
Akani treated my wife.'

'Was it for spiders?' Tina asked.

Sergeant Smugg gave her a sharp look. 'No,
actually she had a fear of donuts.'

Tina hastily clapped a hand to her mouth and
stifled a laugh.

'Donuts?' I repeated.

'Yes. She only had to see a donut, and it would make her shake all over and want to run in the opposite direction. I lost count of the number of tea shops I had to leave because my wife had suddenly made a dash for the door screaming, "*Don't let the donuts get me!*"

Mrs Akani treated my wife successfully and now Mrs Smugg can look at a donut without fainting or running off. So your accusation that Mrs Akani is making Mr Okonjo run slowly is, to my mind, totally ridiculous. Goodbye.'

That was the end of our visit to the police. I had one more idea, the very last one. We went back to Tina's and looked on her laptop for the phone numbers of hypnotists.

'It doesn't matter who it is,' I said. 'We just need to speak to one or two.'

'Try this number,' suggested Tina, and I dialled. A man answered. I took a deep breath and went on.

'I just have a question, but it's very important,' I explained. 'I want to help someone who is stuck in hypnosis and wants to get out of it. How can that be done?'

'Well now, of course, the whole point of hypnosis is that it remains deeply embedded in your mind and you don't come out of it at all.'

'Yes, I understand that, but suppose you DO want to get out of it. Can you stop your mind from obeying the hypnosis?'

The hypnotist cleared his throat. 'Normally, the procedure would be for the person who put the hypnotic suggestion in the mind in the first place to undo it. That is the normal practice.'

'Yes, I understand that too, but suppose the

hypnotist had died and couldn't undo it?'

'That doesn't usually happen,' was the reply.

I gritted my teeth. ARRRRRGH! Would I ever get a useful answer?!

'But suppose they did? Suppose for example the hypnotist got run over by a bus?'

'Buses don't normally run people over.'

'JUST IMAGINE ONE HAS!' I yelled, and hastily quietened down. 'Please, how can the hypnosis be broken?'

'Well now,' the man droned on. 'I suppose that if the patient who has been hypnotized has a sudden shock, that might jolt them out of their hypnotic state, but that would only work when the patient was following the hypnotic suggestion.'

'Thank you,' I said, and put down the phone. I turned to Tina. 'We have to go to the International Games tomorrow and, somehow, we have to give Kriss a shock that will make him forget he's been hypnotized. And it has to be done while he's actually racing.'

Tina stared at me with wide eyes. 'Well that's going to be really, really easy, isn't it?' she declared heavily. 'We may as well give up right this minute.'

I fell back on Tina's bed and stared at the ceiling. How could we possibly shock Kriss, and do it while he was actually in a running race? What were we supposed to do?

'We could stand at the side of the track and throw something at him?' I murmured.

'Throw what?' Tina asked.

'I don't know. Our shoes? Our packed lunches?'

'People will love that,' Tina said. 'We'd be arrested in no time at all and get thrown out. Your mum and dad won't be very pleased when that happens, will they?'

'It's ridiculous,' I grunted. 'Kriss really thinks he's going to run faster than ever and it will actually be slower than ever. It's so unfair.'

Tina was silent for a few moments. Then she just said, 'Mmmmm.'

'Mmmmmm what?' I asked.

'You know what you said about throwing our packed lunches at Kriss. Do you think that would work?'

I sat up. 'Probably not. I was joking.'

'I know. But it would be a big surprise.'

We both chuckled at the idea of hurling sandwiches at the passing runners. 'It would be a bit like when Kriss sat on that pizza and Streaker chased —' My voice died in my throat. We looked

at each other and at the same moment we grabbed each other's shoulders.

'Streaker!' I shouted. 'We don't throw sandwiches. WE THROW STREAKER! We take her to the International Games and as Kriss goes past we let go of Streaker. Kriss is bound to be wearing his lucky running shorts, and they've got pizza stuck all over them.'

'Unless he's washed them,' Tina pointed out.

'It's our only chance,' I shot back.

Tina nodded. 'OK, but how are we going to get Streaker to the Games? Your parents aren't going to let her come with us, are they?'

'No. We shall just have to smuggle her in somehow.'

Tina nodded again. 'Yep. Easy-peasy. Just smuggle a large dog into the International Games. As you do.'

We both groaned in despair and fell back on to the bed.

11. Mrs Akani Strikes Back!

In fact the first part turned out to be pretty
simple. We put Streaker into Tina's biggest bag.
All we had to do was hide her head whenever my
parents were around and make sure she could
breathe. Because it was Tina's bag, they didn't
ask any questions, though my mum did give Tina
a funny look and say she thought Tina must
be carrying an awful lot of packed lunch if she
needed a bag that big.

'It's got my coat in it as well,' Tina told her. 'In case it rains.'

Streaker thought hiding in Tina's bag was great fun. The problem was that she wanted to play Getting In And Out Of The Bag even more. It was a bit of a struggle at times. However, we were already in the car and on our way to the Games, so Tina and I were pretty happy. We sat in the back of the car with our fingers, legs, toes, ears, eyes and almost everything else crossed for good luck.

Then Streaker began whining.

'What was that noise?' demanded Dad.

'What noise?' I asked.

'That whiny sort of noise.'

'It was the wind on the side of the car, I think,' I suggested, just as Streaker did it again.

Dad grunted. 'Sounds more like Streaker, if you ask me. We haven't got Streaker on-board, have we?' And he laughed, because he was joking, and I laughed and pretended to agree with him.

'Yeah, where's Streaker? Is she under the bonnet, Dad?'

'No, she's clinging on to the roof with all four paws,' joked Dad. 'Ha ha ha!'

Streaker suddenly stuck her head out of the bag and went 'Ooooooo!'

'That was Tina,' I said hastily. 'I think she's pretending to be Streaker.'

'Ooooo!' went Tina, obligingly.

The trouble was, I knew what that whine meant. What Streaker was trying to say was: 'I want to do a wee-wee!'

I frantically whispered to Tina. 'We've got to get Streaker out of the car and out of the bag so she can do a wee.'

Tina whispered back. 'What are we going to do? Point her out of the window?'

'Don't be daft! You pretend you need the loo and take her with you!'

'Trev, when I go to the loo I don't take a large bag with me, especially if it's got a dog in it.'

'Well you're going to have to this time,' and before Tina could stop me I reached forward and tapped Dad on the shoulder.

'Sorry, Dad, can you stop soon? Tina needs to, erm, you know.'

'Oh for heaven's sake,' Dad exploded. 'We only left the house half an hour ago!'

'Sorry,' muttered Tina as Dad pulled over.

'You'd better go behind that hedge,' said Mum

as Tina opened her door. 'Do you want me to come with you?'

'I'll be fine,' Tina said.

'Why are you taking your bag? You don't need that.'

'It's got some —' Tina stopped. What was she supposed to say? She couldn't think of anything.

'Toilet paper!' I said quickly.

'You've brought your own toilet paper with you?' asked Mum in amazement. 'Is that what you usually do?'

'Yes,' Tina answered lamely. 'My mum never lets me go anywhere without toilet paper. Just in case.' And she hastily vanished behind the hedge.

Dad turned round and looked at me seriously. 'Trevor,' he said, holding up a warning hand. 'Don't marry her. Any girl who carries toilet paper with her "just in case" must be a bit, you know, crazy-crazy!'

'Dad, she's not my girlfriend,' I told him for

the billionth time, as Tina reappeared. She settled in the car and off we went.

After that there were no more problems. I think Streaker must have gone to sleep. We headed for the Games and soon we were threading our way through the crowds and taking our seats in the huge arena.

It was amazing! The arena was filled from top to bottom with thousands and thousands of people. We were lucky enough to have seats only two rows back. There were loads of events going on, mostly running races. They did the 100 metres, 200 metres, hurdles and all sorts. It was really exciting and we cheered ourselves silly.

Then came the event we had all been waiting for. The 3,000-metre steeplechase was starting and you should have heard us cheer when the names of the runners were announced and they called out Kriss! It was fantastic. The only trouble was that by this time all the cheering and shouting had woken Streaker, who was

desperately trying to get out of the bag
while Tina and I were desperately trying
to keep her in it. We couldn't shut the
bag tight because the poor dog had to
breathe. Besides, we were waiting for
the moment of moments. Luckily it was
almost upon us.

The athletes lined up, the starter

called, 'On your marks!' The gun went
off and so did the runners. They went
pounding past on the first of seven and a
half laps. Kriss Okonjo and Azi Numa were
bunched up in the middle at first but as they
got to the fifth lap they both began to break
for the front. We roared at Kriss as he went
past.

'Go on, Kriss! You can do it!'

Now the pair of them were out at the front on the far side of the track, keeping pace with each other. They came round for the sixth lap. Kriss was beginning to fall back. I could see the strain on his face. He looked so tired! Azi was edging ahead quite steadily. Not only that but Kriss had now been overtaken by three other runners. He was way back in fifth place and still losing ground. This was terrible. Mrs Akani's hypnosis was doing its awful work.

It was time to set loose our secret weapon. 'This is it,' I hissed at Tina. 'Next time Kriss is passing us we have to rush to the front and drop Streaker over the fence.'

'Will it work?' asked Tina.

'Too late to ask that now. It's our only chance. Here comes Kriss. Get ready! Now!'

Tina and I leaped from our seats and clambered over the surprised people in front of us.

'Sorry! Sorry! Sorry! Oops! Sorry!' I called out as we trod on people's legs and laps and shoulders and heads and tumbled and stumbled forward, while they shouted and bellowed at us.

'Oi!'

'Geroff!'

'You clumsy clods!'

We reached the fence and tipped Streaker over the top and on to the track just as the runners were whizzing past. For a moment Streaker just looked at them and everything else around her, and then suddenly she was off. She was running with the runners, leaping and barking.

The crowds in the stand began to laugh and cheer while the dog raced between the runners' legs, and then Streaker must have seen Kriss, or maybe she'd got a whiff of pizza. Suddenly she put on speed. She was running, she was racing and barking, catching up with him. Kriss glanced behind and saw the dog coming for him. Instinctively he put a hand over his bottom to

protect himself. Streaker was after pizza pants!

She was almost at his heels and now Kriss was
lifting his feet higher, taking longer strides. HE
WAS SPEEDING UP! Faster and faster he went,

tearing through the field. He was in fourth place
– third – second, with only Azi Numa in front!

But what was that terrible bellowing going
on? Who was that on the track? IT WAS MRS

AKANI! She was on the running track, waddling after the runners. She had a megaphone in one hand and she was shouting at Kriss.

'YOU ARE FEELING SLEEPY! YOUR LEGS ARE LIKE LEAD! YOU CANNOT LIFT YOUR FEET! THEY ARE STUCK IN CONCRETE! YOU HAVE EATEN TOO MANY JAM PUDDINGS AND CAN NO LONGER MOVE!'

But Kriss wasn't listening. Streaker was snapping at his lucky shorts and Kriss was running faster and faster. The finishing line was coming up and Azi Numa was still in front, but Kriss was catching him and – a huge roar went up from the crowd. The race was over.

But who had won? The finishing line was on the far side of the track and Tina and I couldn't see. We turned to look at the big screen for the announcements. Seconds went by and then the board flickered into life and the result was shown. First place –

KRISS OKONJO!

He'd won! In fact he was still running, with Streaker bouncing along behind him having a great time. I think they were both doing a victory lap.

Mum and Dad seemed very puzzled.

'Where did that dog come from? What's it doing on the track? It shouldn't be on the track. It looks a bit like Streaker. Good heavens – it IS

Streaker! How did Streaker get here? Trevor?
Tina? Where are you? Do you know anything
about this? TREVOR?!'

The Last Bit

Tina and I were in deep doo-doo, but only for a short while. We hadn't even got home when the news came over the car radio.

'Tamsin Plank reporting. There was quite a scene at the International Games today during the 3,000-metre contest between Kriss Okonjo and Azi Numa. Numa was in first place during the closing stages when a dog got on to the track and chased Kriss Okonjo. Okonjo speeded up considerably and overtook Numa with the last strides of the race, also breaking the world record. The dog was caught and returned to its embarrassed owners. The race was also disturbed by Azi Numa's mother, who had apparently hypnotized Kriss Okonjo to run a slow race. Mrs Numa was detained by the police and is now being questioned.'

Tina and I sat in the rear of the car with Streaker between us. (No longer in the bag!) We sat and kept absolutely quiet while my parents listened to the report. Dad switched it off when it was finished, and we drove for the next five minutes in silence. Eventually Dad gave a little cough.

'Um, I think we owe you two an apology. That is what you were trying to tell us, isn't it, and we didn't believe you? I'm sorry about that.'

I tapped Dad on the shoulder. 'That's OK,'
I told him. 'You can't be right all the time, can
you?'

Dad's eyes narrowed. 'No, Trevor, I can't.
But please don't get too carried away by that
thought.'

Tina and I started giggling.

So that was *that* problem solved. All we had to
do now was get through the Animal Games, and
that meant facing Charlie Smugg, not to mention
his three Alsatians, and Chips the Wonder Collie.

The very next day I washed Streaker and
combed her until she looked as smart as a new
kettle — smooth and shiny and ready to boil. The
races were being held at the football ground and
it was crowded with people and their pets.

The running race came up first. Charlie and
Sharon were showing off Lamborghini and a
small crowd had gathered round. Sharon's dog
was not only powerful but looked every inch
a winner. He was a pure pedigree with lovely

long legs and graceful lines. I was annoyingly surprised. All along I had wanted to hate the dog because it was Charlie and Sharon's, but I had to admit he was in fact rather splendid and beautiful. In comparison Streaker was smaller and shorter and most definitely a mongrel. If Streaker was going to lose, at least she would lose to a worthy opponent.

'Fat chance you've got,' chortled Charlie when he saw us. 'You're going to be left dead in the water.'

There were twelve dogs up for the speed race.

We had to stand with our dogs on the starting line and wait for the signal. A fat man with a bald head acted as starter.

'I haven't got a starting pistol,' he apologized. 'So I shall call out – ready, steady, bang! Understood? Right then, READY – STEADY – BANG!!'

And they were off – well, most of them at any rate. Three dogs were far more interested in sniffing each other, the way dogs do. The other nine were belting along, with Lamborghini cruising in front with long, graceful bounds.

Behind him Streaker looked a bit like a frantic spider, trying desperately to keep up. A wave of pity came over me. Poor Streaker. Why had I taken up that wretched challenge? She was busting a gut out there for me and she was going to lose.

They reached the first bend and I noticed a curious thing: all the dogs began to slow down as they rounded the bend, which was pretty tight – all the dogs except Streaker, who just carried on at full speed. That's what she has always done. She has very powerful legs, but they are not all that long and she has always been brilliant at cornering.

Along the straight bits of track Streaker was losing ground to Lamborghini, but on the bends she was making it up again. All in all they were keeping pace with each other.

'Come on, Lambo!' bellowed Charlie.

It was the last corner, and the greyhound felt Streaker on his tail. He went into the corner fast.

His paws lost grip, he scrabbled madly, then fell, tumbling over, while Streaker shot past and into the home straight. Lamborghini was back on his feet and loping after her, catching her with his whopping great strides, but it wasn't enough. I couldn't believe it. Streaker had won.

MY DOG, STREAKER, HAD WON!

MY DOG! MY WONDERFUL, WONDERFUL STREAKER!

Charlie fixed me with the most nasty stare.

'You wait,' he hissed. 'There's still the frisbee competition, and I'm going to murder you. I'm going to murder you AND your stupid dog!'

If you hadn't noticed yet, Charlie's not very nice.

Tina was wearing the biggest smile ever. She flung her arms round Streaker and smothered her. 'You are the best!' she cried. Then she jumped up and flung her arms round me! Aaaargh! 'And you are the best too!' she squeaked, and kissed me! On my cheek! IN FRONT OF EVERYONE! Double aaaargh!

'Come on,' I said quickly. 'The frisbee competition is about to start.'

There were only five dogs in this. Streaker, all three of Charlie's Alsatians and Chips, Tim's wonder collie. Chips was bouncing about, waving his very fluffy tail as if to say: 'Ha ha, aren't I the most wonderful creature on this earth! Just look at my lovely fur all washed and brushed. Aren't I the handsome one! Aren't I the most lovely! Oh do look at me!'

And if Charlie's Alsatians could speak, they were saying: 'Gonna bite your heads off, all of you! So watch out!'

And if Streaker could speak, she would have been saying: 'Any pizza anywhere? Please say yes!'

The frisbee competition was a real challenge. There were going to be six throws altogether, and whichever dog got the frisbee most often would be the overall winner.

The fat, bald-headed starter came over with

a large, yellow frisbee and explained all this.
He asked us to line up our dogs. 'As soon as the
frisbee leaves my hand, you can let your dog go,'
he told us. 'Ready, steady –'

'Are you going to say "bang" again?'
interrupted Tim.

'No, son. This time I shall say "woosh", which
I think is more suitable for a frisbee. Here we go.
READY, STEADY, WOOOSH!'

The frisbee went sailing off with five dogs

 after it. To my
astonishment
Streaker was out in
front. She leaped up,
seized the frisbee
and came trotting
back. Unbelievable!

'One to Streaker,'
announced the
starter. 'Here we go again. Ready,
steady, woosh!'

Off went the frisbee, and this time Chips strutted his stuff and got it, while Streaker went off to examine the starter's left shoe for some strange reason.

The frisbee was thrown for the third time and this time I saw out of the corner of my eye something drop from Charlie's hand. Off went four of the dogs while Streaker sniffed at a large piece of chocolate lying near Charlie's feet. The cheat! He'd deliberately thrown food down to distract Streaker! Streaker snaffled it quickly and sat back, looking very pleased. Meantime, one of Charlie's Alsatians

had seized Chips by the tail while the other two got the frisbee between them and brought it back.

'So we have one fetch for each contestant,' said the starter. 'Here we go for the fourth launch. Ready, steady, woosh!'

The frisbee sailed out. Streaker went charging ahead but this time she had seen a butterfly and off she went, jumping and barking while one of Charlie's Alsatians collected the frisbee. Chips had run a bit and then given up. I don't think he could bear to sustain any more damage to his splendid tail. After all, it would ruin his looks if it got bent or something even worse. Tim patted his dog sadly.

'I'm not taking part any longer in the competition,' he announced. 'I don't wish my dog to be hurt.'

I went across and told Tim I was sorry he was withdrawing. He glanced at Charlie's Alsatians.

'It's not your fault, Trevor. You know how it is with some people. Good luck!'

On the fifth launch Streaker suddenly seemed to get herself back into gear. She streaked ahead of Charlie's dogs, grabbed the frisbee and brought it back, despite an attack launched on her by two of the Alsatians. There was an awful lot of barking and the fight had to be broken up.

'You'd better keep your dog under control,' seethed Charlie.

The starter looked at Charlie sternly. 'Young man, that attack was clearly provoked by two of your dogs. Be careful you are not disqualified. This will be the last throw. Two dogs are tied on two fetches each. May the best dog win. Ready, steady, wooosh!'

I couldn't believe my eyes. Charlie did it again! A lump of chocolate fell to the ground, right in front of Streaker. She bent down and sniffed it while Charlie's dogs were off after the frisbee.

'Go, Streaker, go!' I yelled. She looked up at me, glanced after the disappearing Alsatians, eyed the chocolate one more time then shot off after the frisbee.

'GO!' I screamed after her, while Charlie just stood there going, 'Hurr hurr hurr!'

The Alsatians were well ahead and the frisbee was still high in the air, but slowly beginning to sink. Charlie's dogs galloped after it, and after them came Streaker. I knew she couldn't leap as high as the Alsatians, but she could outrun them and she was catching them fast – but the frisbee was now descending fast too.

Down it came, and the leading Alsatian leaped into the air, rising, rising, jaws ready for the frisbee. Streaker could never jump that high, but now she was leaping too. Oh my goodness! I had to hold my breath. Streaker leaped into the air, and then leaped again OFF THE LEADING ALSATIAN'S BACK! She used Charlie's Alsatian like a stepladder to the frisbee, grabbed it and came hurtling back, to enormous cheers!

'That's cheating!' fumed Charlie. 'That's not allowed. That dog's disqualified! Call the police! I want that dog arrested for cheating!'

The crowd began laughing and a very stern starter strode across to Charlie. 'Young man, I am the judge here, not you, and Streaker has won the competition fair and square. Now then, shake hands, and be done with it!'

Charlie had to shake hands with me! Hurr hurr hurr!

He went home absolutely seething with rage. He wouldn't even speak to Sharon, who tottered after him, calling, 'Charlie, talk to me, Charlie!'

Meanwhile Tina hugged me for the second time that day. She even tried to kiss me again but I managed to duck and she only got the top of my ear.

So it was all over. Kriss Okonjo had a gold medal, a world record and some pizza stuck on his lucky running shorts. Streaker had two gold medals and some chocolate she hadn't expected.

And what did I have? The best dog in the whole world, that's what. And the best friend too. (Friend, not GIRLfriend.)

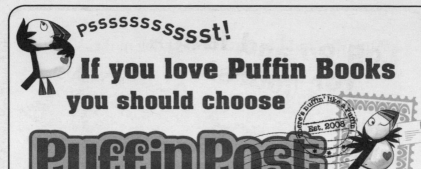

It all started with a Scarecrow

Puffin is well over sixty years old.
Sounds ancient, doesn't it? But Puffin has never been
so lively. We're always on the lookout for the next big
idea, which is how it began all those years ago.

Penguin Books was a big idea from the mind of
a man called Allen Lane, who in 1935 invented
the quality paperback and changed the world.
**And from great Penguins, great Puffins grew,
changing the face of children's books forever.**

The first four Puffin Picture Books were hatched in 1940 and the
first Puffin story book featured a man with broomstick arms called
Worzel Gummidge. In 1967 Kaye Webb, Puffin Editor, started the
Puffin Club, promising to **'make children into readers'**.
She kept that promise and over 200,000 children became
devoted Puffineers through their quarterly installments of
Puffin Post, which is now back for a new generation.

Many years from now, we hope you'll look back and
remember Puffin with a smile. **No matter what your age
or what you're into, there's a Puffin for everyone.**
The possibilities are endless, but one thing is for sure:
whether it's a picture book or a paperback, a sticker book
or a hardback, **if it's got that little Puffin
on it – it's bound to be good.**